KiYOMi

Written by: Stephen Cosgrove
Illustrated by: Robin James

A Serendipity Book

PRICE/STERN/SLOAN
Publishers, Inc., Los Angeles
1984

SECOND PRINTING — JULY 1984

Copyright© 1984 by Price/Stern/Sloan Publishers, Inc.
Published by Price/Stern/Sloan Publishers, Inc.
410 North La Cienega Boulevard, Los Angeles, California 90048

ISBN: 0-8431-1164-X

Dedicated to the real Kiyomi, who came one day and stole my heart away.
Stephen

In the magical mists where all the oceans of the world came together was a mystical island of shaded jade. The streaming beams of sunlight would glisten on the blossoms of a hundred thousand cherry trees whose beauty bloomed for all to see. This was the island of Mitsu-Kami.

Near the very center of the island stood a meadow that encompassed all the beauty around it. The cherry blossoms danced in the soft, gentle breezes across the meadow, creating a blizzard of snowy petals.

On the side of the meadow nearest the rising sun lived the dancing deer of Mitsu-Kami. As deer go they weren't very tall, but they could leap so high that their movements seemed as graceful as a sunlight ballet.

The most beautiful of the dancing deer was Kiyomi. Her eyes were like large almonds resting in deep still pools. Her fawn-like fur had a silvery tint that reflected the other glories of the meadow. Her feet were cast in black velvet and wherever she walked the meadow grasses seemed to whisper her name . . . Kiyomi.

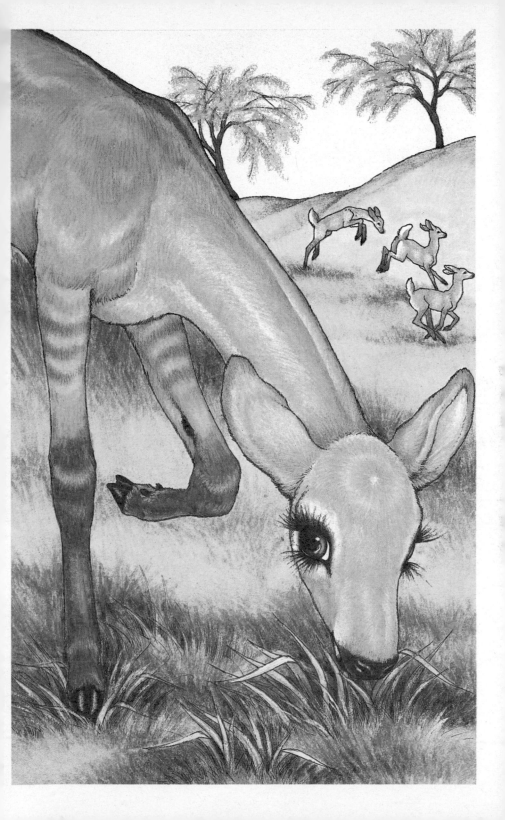

There was no question who was most beautiful amongst the dancing deer; they all knew that Kiyomi was. She knew it and the other deer knew it. Her beauty was as simple as that. Each day she would wander on her side of the meadow, and as she walked past the other deer would comment on how beautiful she was.

"My," they would say, "doesn't Kiyomi's coat reflect the morning mist," or "Don't her eyes shine in the bright chill dawn?"

Occasionally Kiyomi would find herself at the pool at the edge of the wood, where she would gaze in rapt wonder at her own reflection. She would turn this way then that, watching the shadows slip across her fur like a soft, gentle blanket. She had to admit that the other dancing deer were right; she was the most beautiful creature in the meadow.

On the other side of the meadow, winds away from the dancing deer, were the caves of the fire lizards of Mitsu-Kami. They were long, graceful creatures whose scales were colored the dusky fire shades of the setting sun.

The most beautiful of the fire lizards was Sumi. His scales, like flakes of mica and gold, danced with the night light. His eyes flashed a bright, intense blue that brought even the color of the sky to shame. As he would gracefully slither from rock to rock the winds would call his name . . . Sumi.

The other fire lizards were in awe of Sumi. Sumi knew he was beautiful and the others knew he was beautiful; it was as simple as that. As he would glide by, the other fire lizards would stop whatever they were doing to bask in his splendor.

"My," they would say in hoarse whispers, "Did you see how the light seems to dance like the flicker of a flame on Sumi's scales?" or "his eyes are so bright that the sun almost refuses to shine."

Sumi's head wasn't turned by all the compliments. He was magnificent and he knew it. It was just fact.

On occasion, if time allowed, Sumi would wander to the edge of the still waters near the caves. There he would gaze in awe of his own beauty.

He would turn this way and that watching the light skip and dance across his diamond shaped scales. The other fire lizards were right: He was the most majestic creature in the meadow . . . or so he thought.

One day the two most beautiful creatures of Mitsu-Kami met quite by accident at the center of the meadow. As was the custom for both of them, each paused, waiting for the anticipated compliments. The two of them waited and waited, Kiyomi on one side of the trail and Sumi on the other, but nothing was said.

"Hmmm!" they both thought, "Maybe the other is not seeing me in my best light!" So, carefully, they changed places on the trail and waited and waited, but neither one spoke.

"Excuse me," said Kiyomi. "Did you want to comment on my beauty or did you wish to look some more?"

"Well," chuckled a bemused Sumi, "I was thinking the same thing. Did you want to look at me some more?"

Kiyomi was shocked. "Why would I want to look at you? You're nothing but an old lizard!"

Sumi's eyes widened in surprise. "Nothing but a lizard! Who would want to look at a moth-eaten ball of fluff like you?"

So they both stood, glaring at each other, their features twisted in anger. They stood and they watched and they waited.

Time ticked away as the two creatures stood angrily facing each other across the trail. "Well, it's obvious," said Kiyomi, finally breaking the silence, "that one of us can't see his own reflection!"

"Yes!" sneered Sumi. "It is very obvious that one of us can't see her own reflection! Why don't we go together to the mirrored pond at the center of the meadow. There we shall see what we shall see as the sun sets into twilight!"

Kiyomi thought this was a simple solution to Sumi's lack of insight but she insisted that she be seen in the early light of the rising sun. They argued a bit and then both agreed that they would spend the day together so they could see each other in their best light.

Satisfied that the question of beauty would soon be resolved, they headed for the mirrored pond, Kiyomi leaping down the trail with Sumi striding majestically beside her.

They waited at the edge of the pond, each on one side. As the waning light of dusk glittered and skipped across the water it reflected on Sumi's scales like a thousand diamonds in candlelight. But the light also gently caressed Kiyomi's soft, velvety fur.

They stood, nearly frozen in place throughout the night, waiting for the final test. Then, its rays like bright golden ribbons, the sun rose from the east. The light danced across the water, reflecting off Kiyomi in all her beauty and splendor. But the light also glittered in the bright blue eyes of Sumi.

Finally, both were satisfied. They turned away from each other to go back to their own parts of the meadow. They didn't speak to one another as they parted. Sumi didn't want to embarrass the silly dancing deer. After all, it would be hard for her to admit that he was more beautiful than she—but she had seen his reflection.

Kiyomi had to chuckle as she walked away from the poor little lizard. It would be so hard for him to admit that she was more beautiful than he, but he had seen her reflection.

Because they were so absorbed with themselves, what neither of them saw was the tiniest, most beautiful mouse in all the meadow quietly gazing at her perfect reflection from the grass at the edge of the pond.

As you gaze at your reflection
In the mirror above your shoulder
Remember—beauty only shines
In the eyes of the beholder.

Serendipity™ Books

Written by Stephen Cosgrove
Illustrated by Robin James

$1.95 each

For a free list of P/S/S titles, send us your name and address.

The above P/S/S titles and many others can be bought at your local bookstore, or can be ordered directly from the publisher. Send your check or money order for the total amount plus $1.00 for handling and mailing to:

DIRECT MAIL SALES

PRICE/STERN/SLOAN *Publishers, Inc.*
410 North La Cienega Boulevard, Los Angeles, California 90048